MATTHEW McELLIGOTT

G. P. PUTNAM'S SONS

G. P. PUTNAM'S SONS

A division of Penguin Young Readers Group.

Published by The Penguin Group.

Penguin Group (USA) Inc., 375 Hudson Street, New York, NY 10014, U.S.A.

Penguin Group (Canada), 90 Eglinton Avenue East, Suite 700, Toronto, Ontario, Canada M4P 2Y3

(a division of Pearson Penguin Canada Inc.).

Penguin Books Ltd, 80 Strand, London WC2R 0RL, England.

Penguin Ireland, 25 St. Stephen's Green, Dublin 2, Ireland (a division of Penguin Books Ltd.).

Penguin Group (Australia), 250 Camberwell Road, Camberwell, Victoria 3124, Australia

(a division of Pearson Australia Group Pty Ltd).

Penguin Books India Pvt Ltd, 11 Community Centre, Panchsheel Park, New Delhi – 110 017, India.

Penguin Group (NZ), Cnr Airborne and Rosedale Roads, Albany, Auckland 1310, New Zealand

(a division of Pearson New Zealand Ltd).

Penguin Books (South Africa) (Pty) Ltd, 24 Sturdee Avenue, Rosebank, Johannesburg 2196, South Africa.

Penguin Books Ltd, Registered Offices: 80 Strand, London WC2R 0RL, England.

Design by Gina DiMassi. Text set in Fontsoup Catalan Boiled. The artist used a combination of pen and ink and digital techniques
to create the illustrations for this book. Library of Congress Cataloging-in-Publication Data   McElligott, Matthew.
Bean thirteen / Matthew McElligott.   p. cm.   Summary: Two bugs, Ralph and Flora, try to divide thirteen beans so that the unlucky
thirteenth bean disappears, but they soon discover that the math is not so easy.   [1. Division—Fiction. 2. Insects—Fiction.]
I. Title.   PZ7.M478448Bea 2007   [E]—dc22   2006026295   ISBN 978-0-399-24535-0

10 9 8 7 6 5 4 3 2 1

First Impression

For Christy
and Anthony

It was a warm summer night.
Ralph and Flora were picking
beans for dinner.

"How many do we have?" asked Flora.

"Looks like twelve," said Ralph.

"I'll pick one more," said Flora.

"DON'T DO IT!"

shouted Ralph.

"Why on earth not?"
asked Flora.

"Thirteen is an unlucky number,"
said Ralph. "Everyone knows that."

"You're being silly," said Flora.

"I am not," said Ralph.

"You are too," said Flora.

"I am not," said Ralph.

At home, Ralph and Flora
spread the beans out on the
table. They made two piles,
one for each of them.
Each pile had six beans.
"Oh, look," said Flora,
"there's one left over.
You take it, Ralph."

"Bean thirteen?" gasped Ralph. "Never! It's bad luck."

"Ralph," said Flora, "please don't make a fuss."

"I'm not eating it," said Ralph, "and you can't make me."

"I have an idea,"
said Flora.
"I'm not eating it,"
said Ralph.

Flora called their friend April.

"April, would you
like to come over
for dinner? We're
having beans."

"I don't understand," said
Ralph. "We're only going to feed
April one bean?"

"Of course not," said Flora.
"We'll make three piles."

Ralph and Flora separated the beans into three piles. Each pile had four beans. There was one bean left over.

APRIL

RALPH

FLORA

"Bean thirteen!" said Ralph. "I told you!"

"That *is* odd," said Flora. "Let's invite Joe too."

"And make four piles," added Ralph, "so it's fair."

But when they made four piles,
there was still one bean left over.

"I don't understand," said Flora.

"I do," said Ralph. "Bean thirteen
is trouble."

"It's just a bean,"
said Flora. "I'll call Meg.
We'll make five piles."

"This better work," said Ralph as they separated the beans into five piles. Each pile had two beans.

This time there were *three* beans left over.

"It's getting worse!" gasped Ralph.

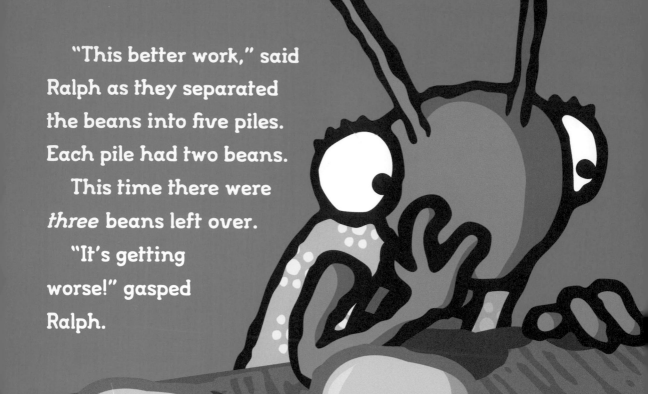

"Don't panic," said Flora. "I'm calling Rocco. He eats everything."

But something still
wasn't right.

"Why does Rocco get
three beans?" complained
Ralph. "That's more than
anyone else."

"Well, we *could* give
him two," said Flora,
"but . . ."

"But what?" said Ralph.
"Never mind," said Flora.
"Tell me," said Ralph.
"But what?"
"It's just that we'll still have an extra bean," said Flora. "I'm really not sure why."

RALPH

FLORA

JOE

APRIL

MEG

ROCCO

"Lousy bean thirteen!" cried Ralph.
"I CAN'T STAND IT!"

DING DONG!

went the doorbell.

"Our guests are here!" shouted Ralph. "What are we going to do?"

He jumped to his feet, he bumped the table, and the beans went EVERYWHERE.

"Oh, Ralph,"
sighed Flora.
"What a mess!"
"Sorry,"
said Ralph.

"Here," said Flora.
"Take this bowl and
gather up the beans.
I'll get the door."

"Hello, everyone!" said Flora. "I'm so happy you could come."

"There are fresh beans in a bowl on the table," said Flora. "Please help yourselves."

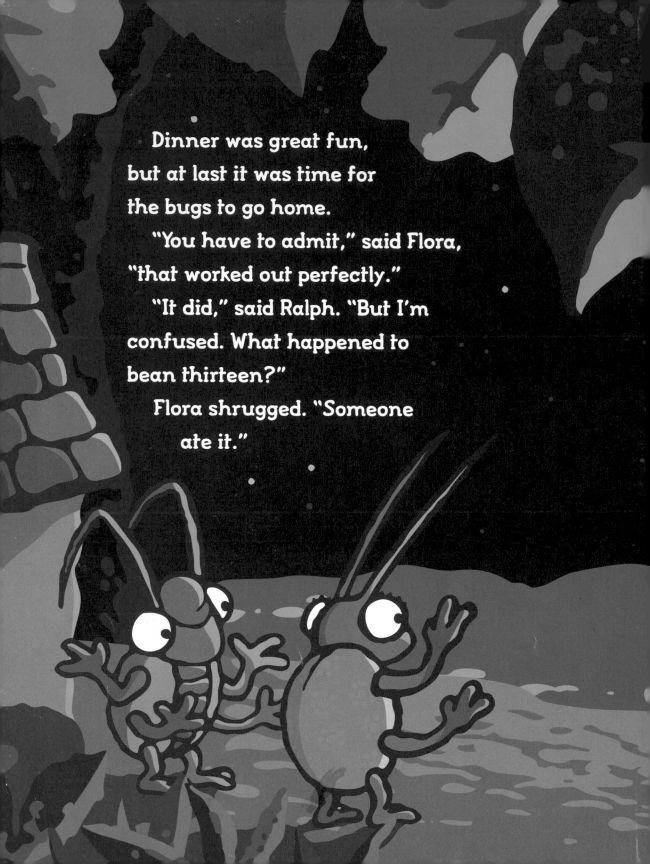

Dinner was great fun,
but at last it was time for
the bugs to go home.

"You have to admit," said Flora,
"that worked out perfectly."

"It did," said Ralph. "But I'm
confused. What happened to
bean thirteen?"

Flora shrugged. "Someone
ate it."

"But who?" asked Ralph. "We'll never know," said Flora. "Maybe April, maybe Rocco, maybe me. Maybe even . . .